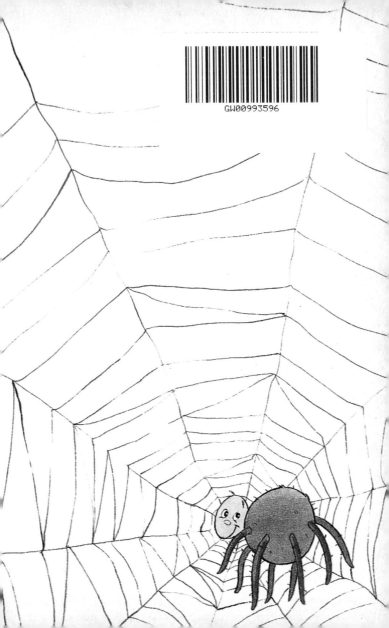

© 1993 Geddes & Grosset Ltd
Reprinted 1994
Published by Geddes & Grosset Ltd,
New Lanark, Scotland.

ISBN 1 85534 585 4

Printed and bound in Slovenia.

The Three Little Pigs

Retold by Judy Hamilton
Illustrated by R. James Binnie

Tarantula Books

There were once three little pigs who had grown just big enough to leave home and make their own way in the world. One sunny day they each packed up their belongings, kissed their mother goodbye, and set off.

"How exciting!" said the first little pig. "I wonder how long it takes to become rich?"

The second pig was more cautious. "It takes a lot of hard work to earn money," he said. "I am going to look for a job!"

The third little pig was the most sensible of all. "The first thing we must do is find somewhere warm and dry to live," he reminded his brothers.

"I am going to build myself a house."

"Now why didn't we think of that?" said the other two.

They carried on down the road for a short distance and then they saw a man stacking straw in a field by the road.

"The very thing!" exclaimed the first little pig, and before the other two could say a word, he rushed over to the man.

"Please could you sell me a bundle of your straw?" he asked the man. The man was only too pleased to sell him some straw.

"I shall be able to build myself a house in no time with this straw!" cried the delighted first little pig. His brothers weren't so sure.

"We want our houses to be stronger than that," they said, "but goodbye and good luck to you."

When his brothers had gone, the first little pig set to work. Just as he thought, it took no time to build his straw house. He got in and shut the door.

"Very cosy," he thought "even if it does wave about a bit in the breeze." Just then, a wolf came along the road.

"Yum Yum! Juicy Pig!" he said sniffing the air. He knocked on the door of the straw house. "Little pig, little pig, let me come in!" called the wolf.

"No, no, by the hair of my chinny chin chin!" cried the frightened pig.

"Then I'll HUFF, and I'll PUFF, and I'll BLOW YOUR HOUSE IN!" the wolf roared. So he huffed and he puffed and he huffed and he puffed. The straw house collapsed. The wolf pounced and ate up the first little pig.

Further along the road, the second and third little pigs came upon a man chopping sticks. The second little pig's eyes lit up.

"Ah! Sticks will make a better house!" he cried, fumbling in his bag for some money. Quickly, he agreed upon a price with the man for an enormous bundle of sticks. The third little pig looked doubtful

"I still think you need to use something stronger than that," he said, shaking his head. But the second pig was determined to build his house of sticks, so his brother had no choice but to let him get on with it. He said goodbye to him and continued on his way.

The second little pig weaved his sticks together and soon he had built himself a little house. He went inside feeling very pleased with himself. The house creaked whenever the wind blew, but the second pig didn't notice. Soon the wolf came along, drawn by the tempting smell of pig. He drooled at the thought of another meal. He knocked on the door.

"Little pig, little pig let me come in!"

"No, no, by the hair of my chinny chin chin!" cried the second little pig.

"Then I'll HUFF and I'll PUFF and I'll BLOW YOUR HOUSE IN!" roared the wolf. So he huffed and he puffed and he huffed and he puffed. The stick house creaked, groaned and fell down. The wolf ate up the second little pig.

The third little pig walked on down the road for a long time. Finally, in a yard at the edge of a village he spotted a man stacking bricks in a pile.

"Bricks," said the sensible little pig to himself, "are heavy and strong and waterproof. I shall build my house of bricks."

He bought an enormous pile of bricks from the man, selected a nice shady spot to build his house, carried all the bricks over to it one by one, and began to build. He was quite sure that his house was going to be stronger than his brothers' houses.

And he was right. It was very hard work, and it was after dark when he finished, but when he got inside and shut the door, his house felt strong and safe. Pretty soon, the wolf smelled the third little pig. He couldn't believe his luck—three little pigs in one day! He knocked on the door.

"Little pig, little pig, let me come in!" called the wolf.

"No, no, by the hair of my chinny chin chin!" shouted the pig bravely.

"Then I'll HUFF and I'll PUFF and I'll BLOW YOUR HOUSE IN!" roared the wolf, just as before. So he huffed and he puffed and he huffed and he puffed. But the brick house stood firm. The third little pig smiled. The wolf had to think of another plan.

The wolf decided to pretend to be friends with the third little pig. He knocked on the door.

"Little pig," he said "there are some lovely turnips in a field near here. Meet me there tomorrow morning at six o'clock and I'll help you pick some!" The clever pig pretended to agree, but got up at five o'clock the next morning instead of six. Before the wolf could get to the field the little pig had picked his turnips and was safely back home. The wolf was cross when he found out about this, but he pretended not to be.

"I'm sorry I missed you at the turnip field today," he said, "why don't we meet tomorrow in the orchard at five o'clock to pick some apples?"

At four o'clock the next morning the pig was in the orchard, up a tree, picking apples. His basket was full and he was about to go home when he spotted the wily wolf coming.

"Little pig," said the wolf, "I see you are early again."

"Yes," replied the pig up the tree, "and these apples are delicious. Here—try one!" He threw an apple over the wolf's head. As the wolf turned round to see where it had landed the pig jumped from the tree and ran home to safety. The wolf followed the pig home and knocked on the door.

"Little pig, would you like to come to the fair?" he said. "Meet me there at three o'clock this afternoon and we'll have lots of fun!"

Once again, the third little pig set off early. At two o'clock he got to the fair and bought himself an enormous butter churn. He set off home down the hill carrying it. Suddenly, he saw the wolf coming up the hill towards him. Quick as a flash, the third little pig dived into the butter churn. The butter churn fell over on its side and began to roll down the hill. When the wolf saw the butter churn clattering towards him down the hill, he was very frightened. He turned and ran away as fast as his legs could carry him. At the foot of the hill, the little pig climbed out of the butter churn, heaved it onto his shoulder and went home.

When the wolf recovered, he went back to the pig's house and knocked on the door.

"I got a terrible fright on my way to the fair," he called. "An enormous butter churn came rolling down the hill after me. It nearly knocked me over!"

"Oh, that was only me," said the little pig cheerfully. "I got inside the butter churn to save myself the trouble of carrying it down the hill!"

The wolf could no longer hide his anger.

"I have had enough of your tricks little pig!" he snarled. "I ate up the first little pig, I ate up the second little pig, and now I'm going to eat YOU! I'm going to climb down your chimney and GOBBLE YOU UP!"

With that, the wolf began to climb up the roof.

The third little pig was frightened, but he was clever and acted quickly. There was an enormous pot of water hanging over the fire, so the little pig quickly put more wood on the fire and stoked it until it was burning fiercely and hot. The pot of water became hotter and hotter as the wolf made his way carefully across the roof. The water was boiling as the wolf climbed up to the chimney. The third little pig closed his eyes and listened. He heard the wolf climbing into the chimney, then 'SPLASH!' the wolf fell down into the boiling water and was killed. The third little pig was safe in his house of bricks.

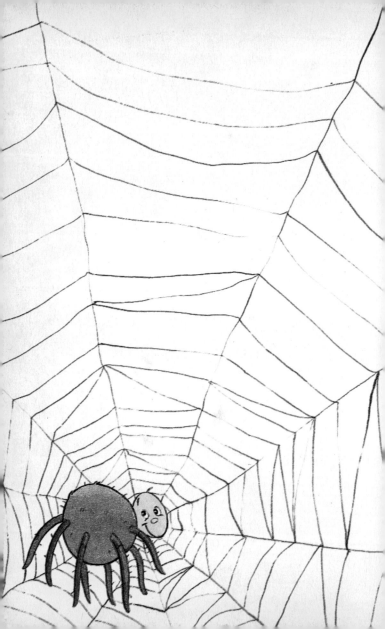